Jack's Fantastic
VOYAGE

Library of Congress Cataloging-in-Publication Data
Foreman, Michael, 1938–
Jack's fantastic voyage/Michael Foreman. — 1st ed.
p.   cm.
Summary: One stormy night Jack experiences an exciting adventure on the sea
with his grandfather but later wonders if it was only a dream.
ISBN 0-15-239496-6
[1. Sea stories. 2. Grandfathers — Fiction.]   I. Title.
PZ7.F7583Jac   1992
[E] — dc20   91-45125

Printed in Italy

A B C D E

Jack's Fantastic VOYAGE

MICHAEL FOREMAN

HARCOURT BRACE JOVANOVICH, PUBLISHERS
San Diego   New York   London

J ack's mother and father both worked in the city, so Jack spent summers with his grandfather, a sea captain, in his house by the ocean.

Jack loved it there.

The house was very old and made of wood. It looked like a beached boat. A strong wind could send sea spray right over the roof and into the narrow street behind.

Yet it was the inside of the house that held the most wonder for Jack. His grandfather had painted pictures everywhere. When he had grown too old to sail the seas he painted his memories. The carved ceiling beams were hung with wooden birds, and the floorboards were carved with fishes. All around the sides of Grandfather's big bed were scenes of wild seas and shipwrecks. On the panel above the pillows was an ocean of icebergs.

At the foot of the bed was mounted a great ship's wheel.

During the day, Jack often played with his friends on the beach, but it was the evenings Jack loved best. That was when Grandfather told him the stories behind the pictures.

Starting out as a young ship's boy, Jack's grandfather had lived a life of adventure. He seemed to have sailed every sea and visited every port.

Jack loved his descriptions of tropical islands, air thick with scents, spices, and parrots. In his imagination he saw great whales spouting, and dolphins and flying fishes leaping around Grandfather's ship.

Most of all, Jack looked forward to stormy nights because then Grandfather told his terrifying tales of typhoons and shipwrecks.

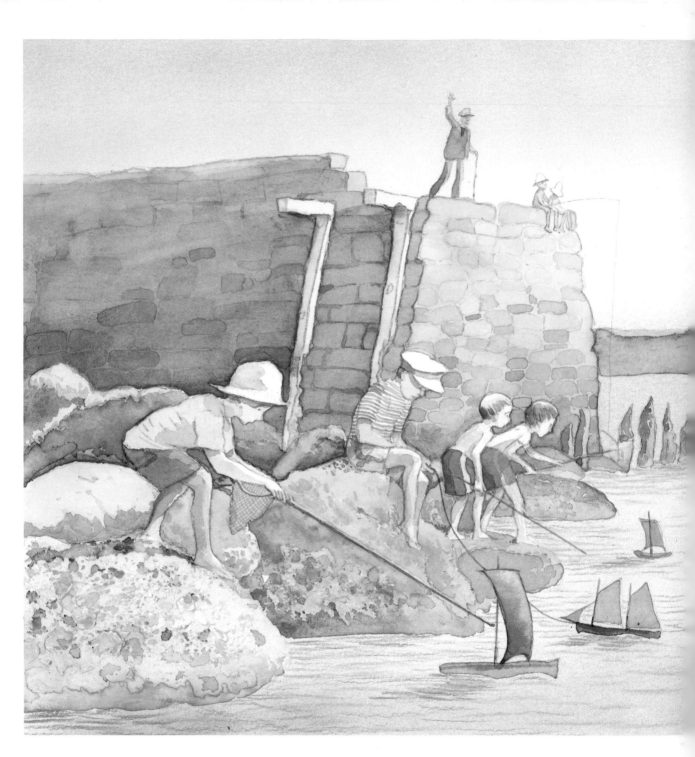

But one day, while playing with his friends, Jack heard some of them laughing about his grandfather.

"Look out, Jack! Here comes your crazy grandad!"

"He's not crazy! I love him," said Jack.

"He is! He's bonkers. Paints mad pictures and makes up stories!"

"He doesn't make them up," cried Jack.

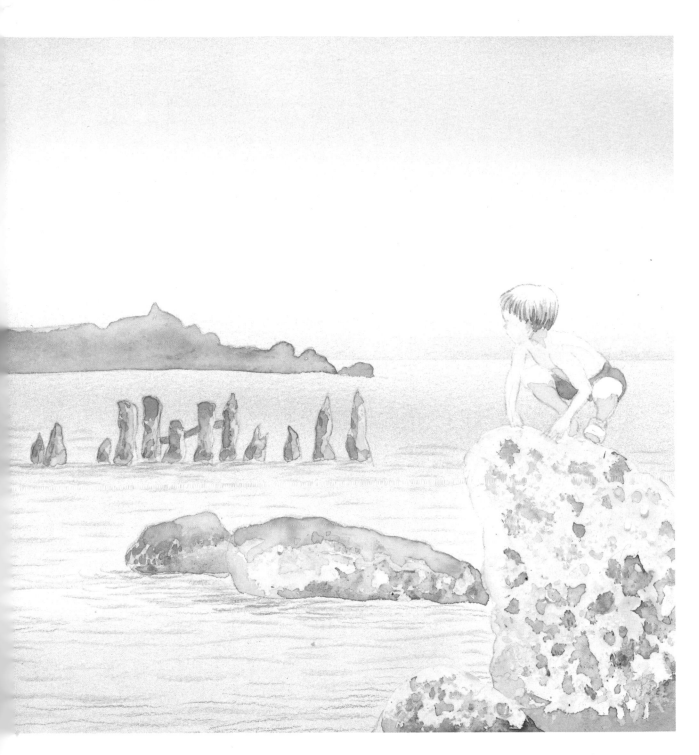

"Of course he does. He's never even been to sea! You ask anyone," shouted one of the boys, and they all ran off as Grandfather approached.

"Had a good time, Jack?" asked Grandfather, smiling. Jack hoped that Grandfather had not heard what the boys had been saying.

That evening, when Grandfather told Jack another story of the sea, he made it sound so real that Jack felt sure he could not be making it up.

Next door to Grandfather's house was a tiny bookshop. The owners were Grandfather's closest friends and sometimes looked after him when he was ill. They often took him bowls of hot soup, but if the bowls were left there too long, Grandfather painted ships all over them.

Surely, thought Jack, they will know the truth about my grandfather.

Next morning, Jack went to the bookshop.

"Well, Jack," said Mr. Andersen, the bookshop owner, "your grandfather hasn't been to sea since we've known him. But he is the oldest person in the village. Maybe he had all his adventures before we met him."

Jack just didn't know what to think.

The next day, Jack didn't go to the beach with the other boys but spent the day on the rocks close to Grandfather's house. Grandfather knew something was troubling him, and that evening he cooked Jack's favorite supper of fish and chips.

When the dishes were washed and stowed away, Grandfather tucked Jack up in the big bed and began another tale.

It was a tale to match the night. A tale of storm and danger amongst icebergs and frozen seas.

The wind was buffeting the shutters, and waves full of stones rattled on the roof. The house shook. Grandfather moved the dishes from the shelves to the cupboards underneath and continued with the story.

"The ship's boy was now at the wheel, trying to hold her into the wind." He turned to Jack. "Take the wheel, Jack." Half asleep, Jack crawled to the ship's wheel at the foot of the bed.

"It was a wild and stormy night!" continued Grandfather. "It took all the boy's strength to keep the wheel steady. Hold her steady, Jack!" he shouted over the storm.

Jack could feel the house shaking, swaying from side to side. Books fell from the shelves and a chair slid across the floor. The storm shutters were now off the windows

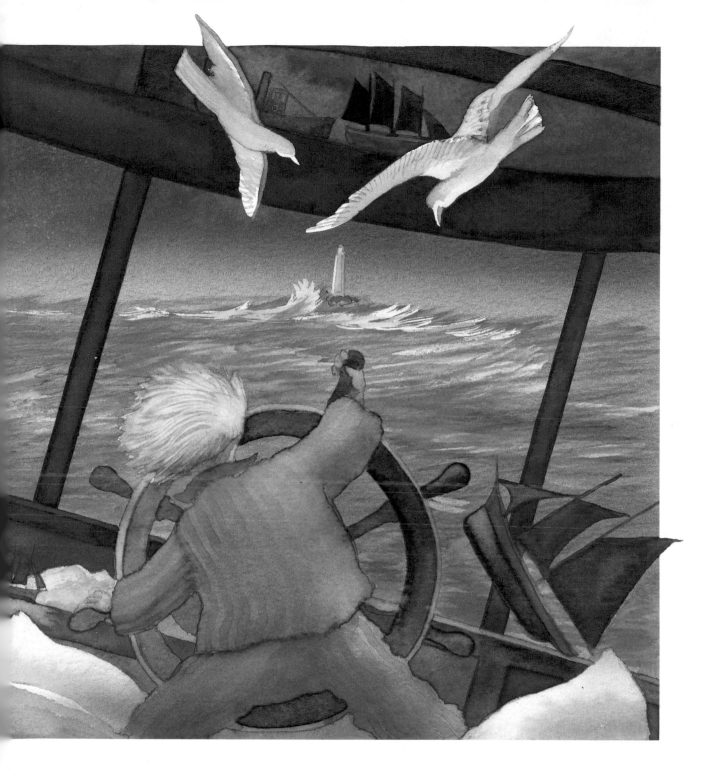

Jack could see the light from the distant lighthouse. It seemed to be bouncing in the dark.

The house was afloat!

Grandfather raced downstairs to the kitchen. Jack heard him
shoveling coal into the big black potbellied stove.
"We need more steam!" he cried. "Keep her steady, Jack!

To the left of the light."

They were beyond the harbor, pitching over the white-topped waves.

As they neared the lighthouse, a thick blanket of fog rolled over them, and only the mournful sound of the lighthouse foghorn told Jack where to steer. It was a comforting sound and reminded him of Grandfather snoring.

Under the fog, the sea was not so rough. Jack began to feel

at ease with the wheel. He got used to the shift and sway. Grandfather was now on the balcony outside the front window, peering into the mist. Sometimes, without turning round, he raised his arm and pointed left or right, and Jack changed course.

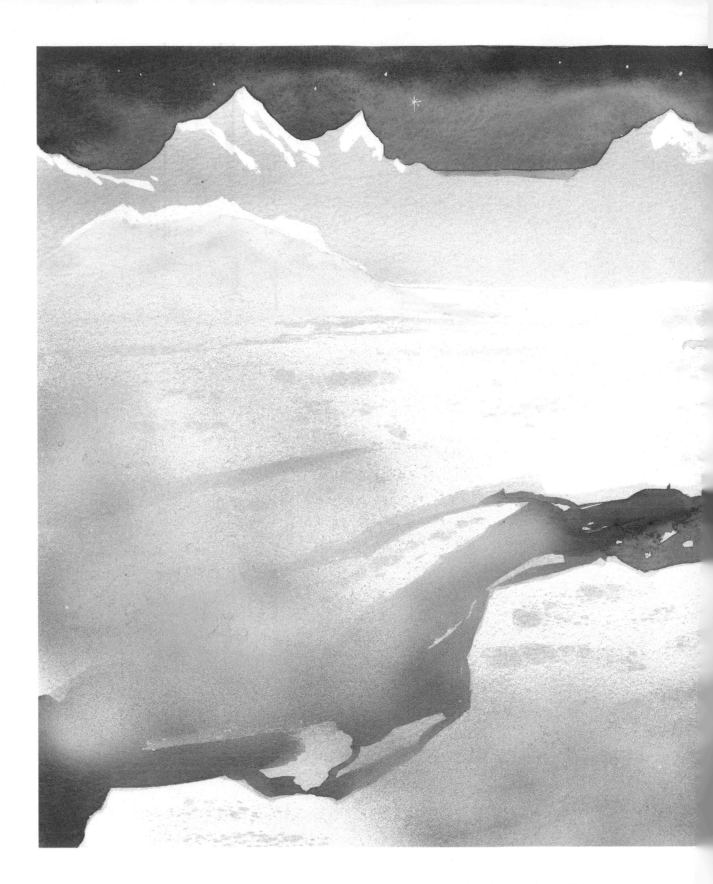

Then the fog thinned and was gone. Instead of black rolling waves, there was a white sea of ice and a sky full of stars.

They sailed slowly through a zigzag channel in the ice until
they entered a blue and green ocean dotted with huge icebergs.

And there they were. All the ships from Grandfather's paintings. The great clippers with their white sails, fast cutters and schooners, brown-sailed smacks and luggers, and even the grimy collier from the coal bucket.

For hours they sailed among this magic fleet, around every iceberg.

Seals were chased by polar bears; whales and narwhals rose
and fell in the clear water.

Then ice began to close over the sea, and the ships were gone.
They sailed back through the zigzag channel and it shut

behind them. The blanket of fog covered everything once more.

When Jack woke up, the pale sun was just appearing over the horizon. He dressed and went out onto the balcony. Everything seemed normal. The house was high and dry among its neighbors.

Had it all been just a dream? Jack went to find his grandfather to tell him all about it.

He found him at the back of the house. Jack could hardly believe his eyes: there was Grandfather standing on a chair, chipping the last telltale icicle off the roof.